KU-312-452

The Tiara Club

at Emerald Castle

Princess Rachel

and the Dancing Dolphin

By Vivian French

ORCHARD BOOKS

The Royal Palace Academy
for the *Preparation of Perfect Princesses*

(Known to our students as "*The Princess Academy*")

OUR SCHOOL MOTTO:

*A Perfect Princess always thinks of others
before herself, and is kind, caring and truthful.*

Emerald Castle offers a complete education for
Tiara Club princesses while taking full advantage of
our seaside situation. The curriculum includes:

A visit to Emerald Sea World Aquarium and Education Pool	*Swimming lessons (safely supervised at all times)*
A visit to Seabird Island	*Whale watching*

Our headteacher, Queen Gwendoline, is present at all
times, and students are well looked after by the school
Fairy Godmother, Fairy Angora.

Our resident staff and visiting experts include:

ABERDEENSHIRE LIBRARY AND INFORMATION SERVICES	
2620141	
HJ	669579
JS	£3.99
JU	JF

*KING JONATHAN
(Captain of the Royal Yacht)*

*QUEEN MOTHER MATILDA
(Etiquette, Posture and
Flower Arranging)*

Aberdeenshire Library and Information Service
www.aberdeenshire.gov.uk/libraries
Renewals Hotline 01224 661511

– 4 OCT 2018

0 4 AUG 2015

1 8 AUG 2015   2 9 NOV 2018

1 8 SEP 2015

1 1 OCT 2016

1 5 MAR 2019

2 2 FEB 2018   0 2 AUG 2019
                2 7 OCT 2022

1 7 MAY 2023

3 1 AUG 2018

                        ABERDEENSHIRE
                        LIBRARIES

                        WITHDRAWN
2 0 SEP 2018   FROM LIBRARY

Princess Rachel and the dancing
dolphin

A L I S

2620141

For Princess Rachel of Malta,
and all her little princesses
xx VF

With very special thanks to JD

www.tiaraclub.co.uk

ORCHARD BOOKS
338 Euston Road, London NW1 3BH
Orchard Books Australia
Level 17/207 Kent St, Sydney, NSW 2000

A Paperback Original
First published in 2008 by Orchard Books
Text © Vivian French 2008
Cover illustration © Sarah Gibb 2008
Inside illustrations © Orchard Books 2008

The right of Vivian French to be identified as the author of this
work has been asserted by her in accordance with the
Copyright, Designs and Patents Act, 1988.

A CIP catalogue record for this book is available
from the British Library.

ISBN 978 1 84616 873 4

1 3 5 7 9 10 8 6 4 2

Printed in Great Britain
The paper and board used in this paperback are natural recyclable
products made from wood grown in sustainable forests. The
manufacturing processes conform to the environmental
regulations of the country of origin.

Orchard Books is a division of Hachette Children's Books,
an Hachette Livre UK company.

www.hachettelivre.co.uk

We award tiara points to encourage our Tiara Club princesses towards the next level. All princesses who win enough points at Emerald Castle will be presented with their Emerald Sashes and attend a celebration ball.

Emerald Sash Tiara Club princesses are invited to return to Diamond Turrets, our superb residence for Perfect Princesses, where they may continue their education at a higher level.

PLEASE NOTE:
Princesses are expected to arrive at
the Academy with a *minimum* of:

TWENTY BALLGOWNS
*(with all necessary hoops,
petticoats, etc)*

TWELVE DAY DRESSES

SEVEN GOWNS
*suitable for garden parties,
and other special
day occasions*

TWELVE TIARAS

DANCING SHOES
five pairs

VELVET SLIPPERS
three pairs

RIDING BOOTS
two pairs

*Swimming costumes,
playsuits, parasols, sun hats
and other essential outdoor
accessories as required*

Hello, best friend! This is me, Rachel.
Do you love parties and balls as much as
I do? When Amelia, Leah, Ruby, Millie,
Zoe and I first heard there was going to
be a Sea Sparkle Ball at our school we
talked about NOTHING ELSE for weeks!
Of course the horrible twins kept telling
us they'd have the prettiest dresses,
but that's just typical of
Diamonde and Gruella...

Chapter One

"Daffodil Room! This must be the THIRD time I've spoken to you, and not ONE of you is paying attention! What ARE you thinking of?"

We jumped guiltily, and I did my best to smile apologetically at Lord Henry. "I'm so sorry," I said. "Er...what was the question?"

Lord Henry rolled his eyes, and sighed heavily. "I was asking if you wanted to travel together when we go to Seabird Island tomorrow."

Of course there was only one answer to that, and we all said, "Yes, PLEASE!"

"Hmm." Lord Henry gave us a stern look. "Just make sure you're all wide awake when we get there," he said. "I'll be asking questions about all the birds I've told you about today, and I do NOT want to find Daffodil Room coming last! You're a very bright group of girls – don't let me down."

"We won't," Amelia promised, but as we filed out of the classroom she whispered, "Oooops! We won't know any of the answers!"

"I wish I'd been listening," Leah said gloomily. "Lord Henry's so nice. I feel awful now."

"Me too," I said, and I meant it. I'd spent the whole lesson imagining myself swooping round the Sea Sparkle Ball in my very best dress, and I hadn't heard a word...

And then I had an idea.

"Maybe we could look it all up in the library?" I suggested. "If we work really hard we might even come first!"

Leah and Amelia nodded, and Ruby, Millie and Zoe made enthusiastic agreeing noises.

"YOU'RE not going to come first in ANY test!" Diamonde pushed past us as we reached the corridor. "WE'RE going to win, aren't we, Gruella?"

"Yes," Gruella said. "WE'RE going to get more marks than ANYONE! WE'RE going to win, and WE'RE going to do the first dance at the Sea Sparkle—"

"SHHH!" Diamonde snapped, and she actually grabbed Gruella and shook her. "I told you not to tell anyone! That's a SECRET!"

Gruella looked as if she was about to burst into tears. "I'm sorry, Diamonde," she whispered, "I forgot."

Diamonde turned on us with a scowl. "She's making it up," she said fiercely. She hauled poor Gruella away, and I could see she was still telling Gruella off as they went towards the dining room.

"GOODNESS!" Zoe stared after them, her eyes wide. "What was that all about?"

Amelia rubbed her nose. "I know a Perfect Princess Never Listens to Gossip," she said thoughtfully, "but I'd say the twins have heard something about the competition..."

"Like, the winner gets to dance the first dance?" Millie nodded. "I think you're right."

"The twins could have got it wrong." Leah took off her glasses, polished them, and put them back on again. "I mean, Queen Gwendoline hasn't said anything about a competition, has she?"

"No." Ruby did her best to look serious. "You're quite right, Leah. All the same…" She gave a little giggle. "Wouldn't it be fun if we were the first dancers on the floor?"

"We've DEFINITELY got to win now," Millie said. "Let's go straight to the library!"

"What about going after school?" I said. My stomach was rumbling in the most unprincessy way, and I knew the lunch bell was about to go. Millie looked disappointed, but luckily Leah and Ruby agreed with me.

"What have we got last lesson?" Zoe asked as we hurried after the twins.

"'Dancing with an Awkward Partner'," Leah said, and she giggled. "Last week I had to dance with Diamonde, and she trod on my toes about a hundred times – and I don't think she meant to!"

"That won't look too good if she gets chosen to open the ball," Amelia pointed out, and we were all laughing as we walked into the dining hall.

Chapter Two

We spent AGES looking up different seabirds that afternoon. Lady Kathryn and Lady Lindsey, who look after the library, helped us find lots of different books and pictures, and Millie filled almost a whole notebook with drawings.

"I do hope we see a puffin," she said as we finally got ready to go.

"They're SO sweet! Just look at their multi-coloured beaks – they look like little clowns!"

Lady Lindsey nodded. "If you go to the cliffs at the end of Seabird Island you might see some," she told us. "They go there to nest in the early summer – but do be careful! The cliffs are quite high."

"We'll definitely go and look," we told her. "Do they nest on the cliff tops?"

Lady Kathryn laughed. "Puffins lay their eggs in burrows. They often stand in the entrance looking pleased with themselves."

We promised we'd look out for
proud puffins, and then we
hurried away to get ready for the
next day. Lord Henry had told us
it was a very early start, and we
were going to have a picnic
breakfast on the boat.

"And we're having a picnic lunch
as well." Zoe sighed happily. "It's
going to be a LOVELY day!"

It didn't feel quite so lovely
when Fairy G, our school fairy
godmother, woke us up the next
morning. It was SO early, and we
all yawned dreadfully as we
struggled out of bed.

"Come along, come along!" Fairy G said cheerfully. "I've been up for hours! Now, don't forget your notebooks and pencils, and everybody remember their parasols. It looks like it's going to be a beautiful day!"

"I'm glad the Sea Sparkle Ball isn't until Saturday," Amelia said as we got dressed. "If it was tonight I think I'd be asleep before it even started!"

Leah grinned at her. "Do you know what? We've been so busy thinking about Seabird Island I'd almost forgotten about the

ball. Have you decided what you're wearing?"

Amelia began to brush her hair. "I think we should wear our very best ballgowns."

"Good idea," Ruby said, and I was just about to say the same when Fairy G banged loudly on our door for the second time.

"You need to be by the front door in five minutes," she boomed, "or we'll go without you!"

We absolutely threw the rest of our clothes on, and zoomed downstairs to find everyone else already there. Fairy G was bustling about giving everyone a paper bag full of delicious things to eat, but when she tried to give Diamonde and Gruella theirs they looked horrified.

"What's this?" Diamonde asked rudely.

"It's your breakfast," Fairy G said. "You can eat it on the boat in the fresh air!"

"But won't there be a cook?" Gruella sounded really whiney. "I wanted toast and scrambled eggs this morning..."

Fairy G began to grow alarmingly large, which is what she does when she's angry. "PRINCESS GRUELLA!" she bellowed, "You have a choice. Either you have a picnic breakfast on the boat, or you don't go!"

Chapter Three

Gruella swallowed hard, and apologised. Even so, I noticed she and Diamonde were muttering to each other as they took their paper bags and went off by themselves into a corner.

"Are we ready?" Lord Henry came striding across the hall, checked the clock on the wall, nodded, and threw the front door open. "Let the adventure begin!" he declared, and he led us out into the chilly early morning air.

We walked briskly along the path to the landing stage – and found a fleet of little fishing boats tied up and waiting.

"WOW!" Amelia gasped. "Are

we going to the island in real fishing boats? That's so COOL!"

Diamonde and Gruella didn't think it was cool at all. I could tell they thought we should be going on Queen Gwendoline's royal yacht, and if Fairy G hadn't been walking right behind them I think they might have made another fuss.

"Let's see," Fairy G said. "Why don't you go with Daffodil Room, Diamonde and Gruella? You can all go on the *Mary Jane*, with Captain Jacob." And she gave us all a huge smile, but I noticed she made sure Diamonde and Gruella were the first to climb on board.

"Pooh!" Diamonde turned up her nose. "It stinks of fish!"

"It IS a fishing boat," Zoe told her. "What did you expect?"

Diamonde didn't answer. She stared out to sea and pretended not to hear as the rest of us found places to sit.

Captain Jacob started the engine while his crew tidied up the ropes, and we started to eat our breakfast. Everything tasted WONDERFUL – Millie said it must be because of the sea air – and although I'd meant to keep some crusts for the seagulls wheeling and calling over our heads I just had to eat every last crumb.

"How long will it take us to get to Seabird Island?" I asked one of the sailors.

"About an hour and a half, Your Highness," he said. Captain Jacob heard him, and smiled at me.

"Were there any special birds you wanted to see?" he asked. "Because if you were wanting to see the puffins, I could take you round the cliffs before we sail into the harbour. We might see some dolphins there as well, if you're lucky."

"Yes PLEASE!" Amelia, Leah, Ruby, Millie, Zoe and I all spoke at once, and Captain Jacob roared with laughter.

"But WE don't want to go round the cliffs," Diamonde said crossly. "Do we, Gruella? WE want to get off this smelly boat."

If Captain Jacob thought she was rude, he didn't show it. "I'll drop you and your sister off first, Your Highness," he said politely.

"You can't get lost on Seabird Island – it's very small. The flowers are beautiful at this time of year, so you can smell all the different varieties!"

Diamonde said something that might have been, "Thank you," and Captain Jacob walked away.

We spent the rest of the trip playing I-Spy, and watching the different kinds of seagulls flying by, or balancing on the rails. Gruella joined in our game, but Diamonde refused to say another word. When we reached the island, Captain Jacob took the *Mary Jane* into a dear little natural harbour made of rocks, and he helped the twins out with a flourish.

"I hope you enjoy yourselves, Your Highnesses!" Captain Jacob called as we moved away again, but only Gruella waved goodbye. Diamonde stalked off without a backwards glance.

Chapter Four

The *Mary Jane* chugged steadily round the island, and we could see how small it was, and how high the cliffs were. We saw LOADS of different seabirds, and Millie ticked them off against her drawings – and then Ruby suddenly gasped.

"LOOK!" She pointed...and we

saw something smooth and silver leap out of the water ahead of us, and then vanish again, leaving a trail of bubbles.

"That there's a dolphin," Captain Jacob told us. "Keep watching – there'll be others keeping it company."

He was right...a moment later another dolphin soared out of the waves, twisted in the air, and dived down. It was much nearer, and we could see its eyes – it looked as if it was smiling.

"That's AMAZING," Leah said. "They're SO beautiful!"

"WOW!" Millie nearly fell out of the boat, she was leaning so far over the rail. "There's a BABY!"

Of course we all wanted to see it, and Captain Jacob turned the *Mary Jane* towards the cliffs, and switched off the engine. The change was amazing; suddenly we could hear the seabirds calling, and the *slap! slap!* of the water against the sides of the boat. There was another *swoosh!* and three dolphins leapt up right beside us – so close that we were spattered with drops of water. Two were quite big – but the third was much smaller, and

as he slid back into the sea
he was making a chirruping
noise that sounded SO happy.

It made us laugh, but the very next moment everything went terribly wrong. The two grown-up dolphins leapt out of the water – but the baby didn't jump with them, and we could see his parents suddenly panic. They dived to look for him, and we held our breath as we waited...and I don't know why, but something made me dash to the other side of the boat, and peer down into the clear turquoise sea.

"Oh!" I gasped. The little dolphin was just below the surface of the water, and he was completely tangled in a fishing net. The other dolphins were anxiously swimming round and round him, but there was nothing they could do.

"Captain Jacob!" I called. "The baby dolphin's here – and he's in trouble!"

The captain came hurrying, and I heard him mutter about, "Idiot amateur fishermen," under his breath as he looked down into the water. He smiled at me, though. "Well spotted, Your Highness," he said. "Now...if we could get a little closer, we might be able to help the poor beast. But I can't start the engine – it would frighten the life out of him."

Ruby came up beside me, and stared in horror at the poor dolphin desperately squirming in an effort to get free of the tangle of ropes. "Suppose someone dived in? Could they rescue him?"

"The splash would make him even more frantic." Captain Jacob sighed. "He'll rub himself raw if he keeps on wriggling like that – and he'll drown if he can't get to the surface to breathe."

I was looking round the deck of the fishing boat, and I suddenly saw a rope ladder folded up under a seat. "What if someone climbed down that?" I asked. "They might be able to reach in and untangle him..."

The captain stroked his chin

thoughtfully. "That might work," he said slowly. "But that ladder's old and worn out. That's why it's on deck. It wouldn't take my weight..."

"But it would be strong enough for me!" I grabbed his hand. "PLEASE let's try! We HAVE to save him!"

There was a tiny pause – then Captain Jacob nodded. "We'll get the ladder tied to the rail," he said. "I'll get you a life jacket and a sharp knife to cut the net...but watch what you're doing!"

Chapter Five

Have you ever climbed down a rope ladder? It felt SO odd – and as I climbed it creaked horribly, and I kept seeing bits where the rope had frayed. I gritted my teeth, and went on down...and as I reached the sea I gasped. It was COLD! But the baby dolphin was really close, so I moved as quietly and gently as I could. If I held on to the ladder with one hand I could almost reach the edge of the horrible net – almost, but not quite. My heart missed a beat as I realised I wasn't going to be able to help. And then I felt a hand seize mine, and there was Ruby just above me.

"Rachel, if I hold the ladder and your hand," she said, "you can lean out further." Ruby was right. If I leant right away from her I could touch the net. Very, very gently I began to cut the tough strands, and all the time I kept murmuring, "It's OK, little dolphin – it's OK. Please don't be frightened..."

And then the weirdest thing happened. The dolphin stopped struggling, and stayed incredibly still, and it was SO much easier.

One strand snapped after another as I sawed away – and at last the baby was free!

"PHEW!" I said, and I suddenly realised my arm was aching horribly. It didn't matter, though, because something smooth and silvery and beautiful had swum

right up to me, and was making cheery little clicking sounds as if to say "Thank you! Thank you!" And then, before I had time to say anything back, the mother dolphin had collected her baby and hurried him off towards the open water...

Next moment I heard cheering! Really loud cheering.

Ruby and I looked up, and there, watching from the cliffs of Seabird Island, were the other princesses from Emerald Castle.

Fairy G was waving so wildly I thought she might fly away at any moment, and Lord Henry was standing beside her clapping madly. Ruby and I looked at each other, and if we hadn't been balanced on a rope ladder we'd have had a massive hug before we hauled ourselves back on board the *Mary Jane*.

"Well done, Your Highnesses!" As I gave Captain Jacob back his knife he was looking delighted. "I'll make quite sure that whoever left that net there doesn't ever do such a thing again. Now, we'd better get you back to your friends..."

And he started the motor.

As the *Mary Jane* chugged back to the harbour I looked down at my clothes – and I was absolutely soaked, and horribly dirty. My shoes were sopping – but do you know what? I didn't care. I kept thinking of the way the dolphin had come to me, and I was SO happy. When we reached the harbour Fairy G was waiting, and she actually laughed when she saw me and Ruby step out of the boat.

"What a pair of soaking heroes," she said, and waved her wand...and we were as spick and span as if we'd just that moment got dressed!

and the Dancing Dolphin

"Right!" Our fairy godmother suddenly sounded very brisk, and we looked at her in surprise. "Captain Jacob will be here to take you home this evening. Now it's time to listen to Lord Henry! We can't have you missing out on your test!" And then she gave us an enormous beaming smile. "But you did very well, my dears. You did very well indeed!"

Chapter Six

The rest of the day on Seabird Island was SUCH fun. Lord Henry showed us lots of different birds, and we recognised almost every one. Every single time we answered a question correctly Diamonde and Gruella gave us sly little sideways looks, and I knew they were worrying about the competition. They knew a lot about seabirds, though – and when they got a right answer they looked SO pleased with themselves!

At the end of the afternoon Lord Henry asked us all to sit down on the grass at the top of the cliffs while he announced the results.

The twins sat up very straight, and folded their arms as if they just KNEW they'd won.

"You've all worked very hard today," Lord Henry told us, "and I'm very pleased. As far as the competition goes, we have a tie. Both Daffodil Room and the twins have the same number of points."

Diamonde absolutely glared at us, but Lord Henry went on, "I'm going to ask you one last question. Who can tell me what bird that is?" And he pointed at a narrow ledge. A small bird was standing looking out to sea, and its beak had stripes of red, yellow and blue – and it had SUCH a funny expression!

Before anyone else could speak, Diamonde's hand shot up. "Easy!" she said. "It's a parrot!"

Amelia put her hand over her mouth, and I saw Millie trying not to smile – but we were all Perfect Princesses, and didn't laugh.

"I'm afraid you're wrong, Diamonde." Lord Henry turned to us. "Daffodil Room – do you know what it is?"

Of couse we did, and we chorussed together, "It's a PUFFIN, Lord Henry!"

"Quite right." Lord Henry

ignored Diamonde as she burst into noisy tears, and he smiled at us. "Well done! YOU will dance the very first dance on Saturday night – and I shall watch with pleasure!"

*

Did we dance the first dance? We certainly did!

The Sea Sparkle Ball was held in the roof garden at the top of Emerald Castle, and it was utterly magic. The evening sun was tipping the clouds with gold, and the waves were whispering and sighing down below as the music began to play.

Our headteacher, Queen Gwendoline, stepped forward to announce that Daffodil Room would have the honour of opening the ball. We tried not to look too proud, but then she went on,

"And I'd like to congratulate these splendid students on yet another remarkable achievement. Today the princesses Rachel and Ruby saved the life of a baby dolphin, without a thought for their own personal comfort or safety.

Perhaps we could ask the two of them to lead their friends on to the floor while we give them a well-earned round of applause?"

I blushed, and took Ruby's hand, and as I did so Fairy G suddenly called out, "Look! QUICK, everybody! LOOK!"

She was pointing over the castle walls, and we all ran to see – even Queen Gwendoline. And there, down below in Emerald Bay, were three dolphins – a mother, a father and a baby – and they

were dancing in and out of the waves and looking up at us with the BIGGEST smiles!

"The dolphins have opened the Sea Sparkle Ball," I whispered to Ruby, and she squeezed my hand.

"They're your friends," she whispered back. "And they want to thank you!"

"Friends look after each other,"

Amelia said as she took my other hand, and Leah, Millie and Zoe gave a cheer from behind us...

And here's another cheer. *Hip hip hurrah!* And it comes with a hug – for YOU!

Don't miss  website at:

www.tiaraclub.co.uk

Keep up to date with the latest
Tiara Club books and meet all
your favourite princesses!

There is SO much to see and do,
including games and activities. You can
even become an exclusive member of the
Tiara Club Princess Academy.

PLUS, there's an exciting
Emerald Castle competition
with a truly AMAZING prize!

Be a Perfect Princess – check it out today!

What happens next?
Find out in
Princess Zoe
and the Wishing Shell

Hi there – I am Princess Zoe,
and I'm SO pleased you're here with us at
Emerald Castle! I don't know about you, but
I find it REALLY hard to concentrate on
lessons when the sun is shining and the sea
is only moments away. I know Amelia, Leah,
Ruby, Millie and Rachel feel the same
way...oh! Have you met them yet? They
share Daffodil Room with me, and
we're all very best friends...

We usually have deportment lessons on Friday mornings, and it can be a bit scary as Queen Mother Matilda takes the class, and she's VERY fierce. As it was getting near the end of term we'd been practising for the Emerald Castle Presentation Day. We were all going to parade up and down the pier before we were given our sashes, and Queen Mother Matilda spent every lesson barking, "Walk for six steps, then TURN! DO try and be graceful, princesses!"

"I'm sure I'll be much too nervous to remember anything on

the day," Rachel said gloomily as we walked towards the ballroom. "I'm really scared I haven't got enough tiara points to win my sash."

"Me too," Amelia agreed.

"Don't even talk about it," I groaned. "The last time I tried to add up my points it came to about thirty, and Diamonde spent the whole of last week boasting that she had at least two hundred."

"Humph!" Ruby made a face. "I think it's a bit unlikely that she's got that many more than you, Zoe."

"That's right." Leah patted me

on the back. "You've probably got LOADS more than her. Perhaps you just can't count!"

It was nice of my friends to be so supportive, but I really was feeling anxious. I'd had a couple of terrible dreams about being the only princess in the whole school who didn't get her Emerald Sash, and I couldn't help wondering if they might be the sort of dreams that came true...

~ Want to read more? ~
Princess Zoe and the Wishing Shell
is out now!

This summer, look out for

Emerald Ball

Vivian French

ISBN: 978 1 84616 881 9

Two stories in one fabulous book!

The Tiara Club books are priced at £3.99. *Butterfly Ball*, *Christmas Wonderland*,
Princess Parade and *Emerald Ball* are priced at £5.99. The Tiara Club books are
available from all good bookshops, or can be ordered direct from the publisher:
Orchard Books, PO BOX 29, Douglas IM99 1BQ.
Credit card orders please telephone 01624 836000 or fax 01624 837033 or visit our
website: www.orchardbooks.co.uk or e-mail: bookshop@enterprise.net for details.

To order please quote title, author and ISBN and your full name and address.
Cheques and postal orders should be made payable to 'Bookpost plc.'
Postage and packing is FREE within the UK
(overseas customers should add £2.00 per book).
Prices and availability are subject to change.